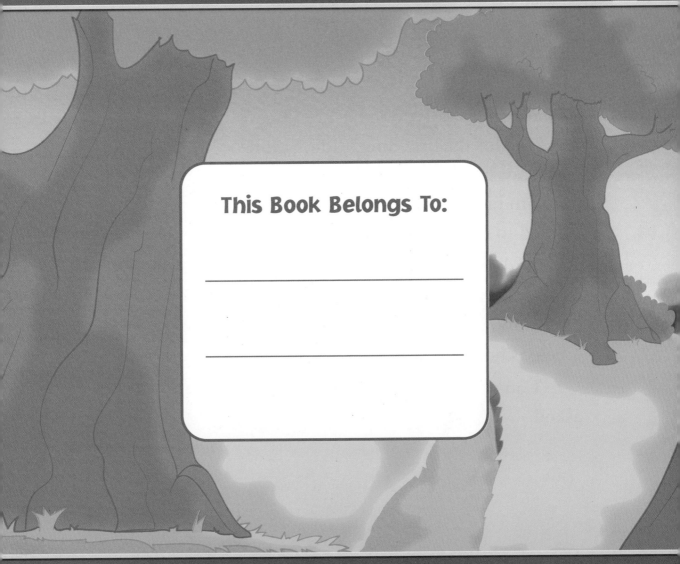

This Book Belongs To:

_____

_____

Randall's New Bike

Randall proudly rode his brand new bike for the first time. Riding alone was okay, but he knew it would be more fun with his friends. Randall really wanted to show them his new bike.

Randall stopped by Benson bear's tree house. He climbed up and knocked on the door. "Hi Randall," Benson greeted cheerfully.

"Can you go bike riding?" Randall asked.

"I have to eat lunch," Benson replied, going over to pour himself a glass of milk.

"Oh," Randall said, disappointed. Looking at Benson's honey sandwich made him hungry. Randall was sure Benson wouldn't mind if he took the sandwich with him.

"Do you want something to eat?" Benson asked, but when he turned around, Randall was gone— and so was his sandwich!

Randall rode his bike to Fluffy's. She was hanging up her ribbons on the clothesline.

"Do you want to go bike riding?" Randall asked.

"I'm too busy," Fluffy said. "I have ribbons to hang."

As Randall rode away, he took a couple of red ribbons at the end of the line. "They'd look great on my bike. Fluffy won't mind," he thought.

Next, Randall went to Buster Badger's. Buster had a "Stay Away" sign, so Randall hid the sign.

Buster opened the door. "Can't you read the…" he began, then saw his sign was gone. "Hmmm. What do you want?"

"You want to go bike riding?" Randall asked him.

"I have to make a new sign," Buster grumbled and shut the door.

Discouraged, Randall rode to Timmy Turtle's. When Randall arrived, he discovered Timmy was busy polishing his shell. "I can't ride bikes now. I don't want to get dust on my clean shell," Timmy told him.

"Alright," Randall sighed, then thought, "My bike is getting dusty. Timmy's polish did shine things up good. Timmy won't mind if I borrow his polish."

POLISH

Randall picked up the polish as he left, then rode to the pond. He wasn't going to ask anyone else to ride bikes. He would just stay at the pond and clean *his* bike.

He was shining up his bike, when Old Blue came by. "A fella with a fine bicycle like that oughta be happy," he said, noticing Randall's long face.

"Everybody's too busy to ride bikes," Randall complained.

"I see Timmy lent you his shell polish," Old Blue observed.

"Oh yeah, well, sort of," Randall said sheepishly.

"Give it back!" a little voice suddenly shouted from the distance. There was Timmy walking with Randall's other friends toward him.

"You stole my polish," Timmy accused.

"I'm sure you took my sign," said Buster.

"There's my ribbons," Fluffy added.

"My honey sandwich disappeared," said Benson.

"Is it true Randall?" Old Blue asked. "Did you take these things without asking first?"

"I was hungry," Randall explained, "I didn't think Benson would mind— I was going to give back the ribbons, Fluffy, and your polish too, Timmy. I'm sorry. I guess I should have asked you guys first."

"What about my sign?" Buster asked.

"I hid your sign in the bush, Buster," Randall replied, ashamed. "I'm sorry. I wanted you to go bike riding with me. I wanted you all to go."

"Let this be a lesson to all of you young fellas," Old Blue said. "Taking without asking is stealing, and not making time for a friend, is not being a very good friend."